W9-AEA-480

Hamster Camp
How Harry Got Fit

Teresa Bateman

Pictures by

Nancy Cote

LOWER SCHOOL LIBRARY
ACADEMY OF THE SACRED HEART
4521 ST. CHARLES AVE.
NEW ORLEANS, LA 70115
(504) 891-1943

Albert Whitman & Company, Morton Grove, Illinois

For Eric, Christopher, and Tyler, who would give
any hamster a run for his money.—T.B.

To Kathy Marek, for all of her good work
with the children at the Highland Pediatric Office,
as well as her ongoing personal advice
to me and my family. Love, N.C.

Library of Congress Cataloging-in-Publication Data

Bateman, Teresa.
Hamster Camp : how Harry got fit / by Teresa Bateman ; illustrated by Nancy Cote.
p. cm.
Summary: Concerned about Harry's weight gain and lack of exercise, his pet hamster arranges for him to
spend a month at a unique camp, where Harry is transformed into someone who understands that
eating right and staying in shape can be fun.
ISBN 0-8075-3139-1 (hardcover)
[1. Camps—Fiction. 2. Overweight persons—Fiction. 3. Exercise—Fiction. 4. Hamsters—Fiction. 5. Magic—Fiction.
6. Stories in rhyme.] I. Cote, Nancy, ill. II. Title.
PZ8.3.B314Ham 2005 [E]—dc22 2004018582

Text copyright © 2005 by Teresa Bateman.
Illustrations copyright © 2005 by Nancy Cote.
Published in 2005 by Albert Whitman & Company,
6340 Oakton Street, Morton Grove, Illinois 60053-2723.
Published simultaneously in Canada by Fitzhenry & Whiteside, Markham, Ontario.
All rights reserved. No part of this book may be reproduced or transmitted in any form or by any means,
electronic or mechanical, including photocopying, recording, or by any information storage and
retrieval system, without permission in writing from the
publisher. Printed in the United States of America.
10 9 8 7 6 5 4 3 2 1

For more information about Albert Whitman & Company,
visit our web site at www.albertwhitman.com.

T 69226

Harry craved his candy.
He adored his pop and fries.
He liked to laze around the house
and hated exercise.

His parents weren't much better.
So tired, when work was through,
it seemed easier to sit
than find healthy things to do.
It hadn't happened quickly.
Just a little every day—
a pizza ordered in (or two!),
TV instead of play.

Now Harry's hamster winced to see
what Harry had become.
The only workout Harry got
was chewing bubble gum!
His room was filled with wrappers—
candy, chips, and soda straws.
So Harry's hamster, Bob, took fate
into his hamster paws.

'Twas June, and school was almost out.
Young Harry couldn't wait.
He had plans for vacation—
lovely plans to vegetate.
He would watch TV all summer,
and eat snack foods by the pail.
Then his parents got an unexpected
package in the mail.
"How odd," they said, "Still, chances
like this don't come every day . . . "

so they told Harry, "Lucky you!
We're sending you away!"
"Not fat camp?" Harry stammered.
Thoughts of grueling exercise—
jumping jacks, long runs, and chin-ups—
made tears well in his eyes.

"NO, no," his parents reassured
their fretting, fearful son.
"You're going off to Hamster Camp!
Oh, you'll have so much fun!"
Harry rolled his eyes. He begged.
He made an awful fuss.
It didn't help. He found himself
aboard the Hamster Bus.
Hamster Bob was quite delighted.
Harry slumped down in his seat.
"Are we there yet?" he whined and wailed.
"And what is there to eat?"

The bus arrived, he rushed outside,
then saw a flash, quite scary.
When he looked down (not very far),
poor Harry was, well . . . hairy!
The campers now were hamsters!
They ran squeaking here and there.
They left their bags, for hamsters don't *need*
labeled underwear.

Pets leaped out from their cages—
joined their owners on the ground.
Then suddenly a whistle blew.
They quickly turned around.

Hearty hamsters, wearing T-shirts,
led the campers all inside.
"We have a month of fun ahead!"
the hamster counselor cried.

"Fun? I don't believe it.
This is AWFUL!" Harry said.
He lifted up his hamster foot
and scratched his hamster head.
Bob hurried Harry to one side
and looked him in the eye.
"It's your choice what you do," he said,
"but please give this a try.
Here's a chance to make a change—
be the best that you can be.
Besides, a hamster's life is cool—
and that's a guarantee!"

At sunrise campers woke up
to the whistle's high-pitched call.
They raced to get to breakfast,
each inside a plastic ball.

Soon they were running over rocks,
and leaping over poles.
They swam at Hamster Hollow,
and they dove down hamster holes.

Their games were just a-mazing.
Harry couldn't get enough.
Soon he found to his astonishment
that he was getting buff!

He even liked to run the wheel—
he'd make that baby twirl,
then hang on tight with all his might
and watch the world a-whirl.
And clambering to campfire
was a nightly hard-earned quest
that, in hamster terms, would be the same
as scaling Everest!

Junk food? He didn't miss it.
TV? He'd rather play.
With Bob he swam and climbed and rolled
all hours of the day.

The meals were tasty—veggie trays,
and lots of fruit and grain.
Harry'd fill his cheeks with nuts—
as much as hamster cheeks contain!

The weeks zipped by at lightning speed.
Then one night, to Harry's sorrow,
the hamster counselor told the group,
"You're going home tomorrow."

Poor Harry groaned, he cried, he begged,
he faked a heart attack.
But nothing worked. The counselor said,
"Your parents want you back."

The bus was waiting in the lot,
the campers climbed inside.
And then a sudden flash of light—
Harry looked down, and he sighed.

The human campers got new belts
to match their trim physiques.
Their pets received camp T-shirts,
and rejoiced in hamster squeaks.

The bus ride home seemed far too short.
They watched the camp recede,
then squeaked and sang and chatted
as they munched sunflower seeds.

Hamster Camp changed Harry's life.
New sport or game—of course he'll try it!
He runs and plays, spends time outside,
and eats a healthy diet.

At first his parents thought his actions
were a little strange.
But they quickly figured out that
they, too, would have to change.
Harry wanted vegetables.
They had to eat them, too!
Harry took them running.
They bought brand-new jogging shoes.
He made them go outside.
Surprise! It turned out to be fun.
They soon were trim and healthy,
just from following their son.

Now Harry's asked his parents for
a first-class postage stamp.
He wants to be a counselor
at next year's Hamster Camp!

Note to Parents

Harry and his family learn that being healthy and active can be FUN! This simple message, however, is often hard to come by in the real world. When we're concerned about our overweight children, we often (intentionally or unintentionally) send them unhelpful messages that keep us all focused on their weight instead of their health. Now we're beginning to understand the need to work more on improving diet and activity habits than on reducing weight. Positive approaches are better for a child's self-esteem and are thought to be less likely to lead to negative effects such as eating disorders.

Kids and their parents need to support each other while working to make lifestyle changes. It's important to consider what it takes to modify a child's diet or activity level: remember that young children don't shop, cook, or even fully control when or where they are physically active. Changes throughout the entire household are required to make a child's healthy lifestyle possible and sustainable.

Parents can promote health for the family by being role models for good habits and by building opportunities for healthy behavior into a child's daily routine. Some basic guidelines for doing this include: at least moderate levels of physical activity every day, eating multiple servings of fruits and vegetables daily, limiting TV to less than two hours per day, and limiting sugar-sweetened drinks. Family plans should include healthy meals and fun outings with plenty of physical activity opportunities.

If you are concerned about your child's weight, it's good to seek clinical help, but don't overlook opportunities to make changes at home, too.

Matt M. Longjohn, M.D., M.P.H.
Executive Director
Consortium to Lower Obesity in Chicago Children
Chicago, Illinois